CAN I GIVE YOU A SQUISH?

EMILY NEILSON

Dial Books for Young Readers

Dial Books for Young Readers
An imprint of Penguin Random House LLC, New York

Visit us online at penguinrandomhouse.com

Library of Congress Cataloging-in-Publication Data
Names: Neilson, Emily, author, illustrator.
Title: Can I give you a squish? / Emily Neilson.
Description: New York : Dial Books for Young Readers, [2020] | Audience:
Ages 3–6. | Audience: Grades K–1. | Summary: Kai, a merboy, loves to
share hugs with his mother, but learns that some friends prefer fin
bumps, tail claps, tentacle shakes, or claw pinches.
Identifiers: LCCN 2019038745 (print) | LCCN 2019038746 (ebook) |
ISBN 9781984814777 (hardcover) | ISBN 9781984814784 (ebook) |
ISBN 9781984814791 (kindle edition)
Subjects: CYAC: Hugging—Fiction. | Personal space—Fiction. |
Mermen—Fiction. | Marine animals—Fiction.
Classification: LCC PZ7.1.N414 Can 2020 (print) | LCC PZ7.1.N414 (ebook) |
DDC [E]—dc23
LC record available at https://lccn.loc.gov/2019038745
LC ebook record available at https://lccn.loc.gov/2019038746

Printed in China

ISBN 9781984814777

10 9 8 7 6 5 4 3 2 1

Design by Mina Chung • Text set in Eames Century Modern

This art was created digitally.

Dedicated to my moms

Kai gave his mama a big squish.

"I love giving squishes!" he said.

The rest of the morning, Kai gave out squishes.

He squelched some kelp,

and squashed a rock,

and scrunched some buried treasure.

He even gave his friends a big group squish.

Then Kai saw a little puffer fish he wanted to squish.

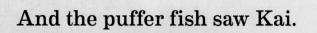

And the puffer fish saw Kai.

SQUISH!

Suddenly the fish puffed up like a big water balloon,
which is what puffer fish do when they are scared or upset.
"I do not like to be squished," said the fish.

Kai felt terrible. All he had wanted to do was give a
friendly squish. But it had gone horribly wrong.
The fish had not liked the squish at all.

"Maybe there is something else you can give besides a squish to show that you want to be friends," said the crab.

But what?

The friends thought. And they considered. And they pondered. Until at last it came to them!

The puffer fish was still hiding when Kai swam up.

"Excuse me," said Kai. "I see you don't like squishes. Would you like a fin bump instead?"

The fish became calm.

"I like getting fin bumps!" said the fish.

"And I like giving them," said Kai.

"What about you guys, what do you like?"

"I like to do tail claps," said the dolphin.
"Me too," said Kai.

"I like tentacle shakes," said the octopus.
So Kai gave him one.

"Does anybody want a claw pinch?" asked the crab.

"Maybe just a little one," said the octopus.

That's when Kai realized,
"Every fish likes their own kind of squish!"

Kai went to find his mama to show her what he had learned.

He gave her a fin bump,

and a tail clap,

and a tentacle shake,

and even a claw pinch.

"Thanks, bubble, but I think I would rather have a squish."

"Okay, Mama."
And Kai gave his mama a great big squish.